I0460919

FRACTURED ERA: LEGACY CODE PREQUEL

BETTER WORLD

AUTUMN KALQUIST

Diapason Publishing

Diapason Publishing
www.AutumnKalquist.com

ISBN-13: 978-0692468517
ISBN-10: 069246851X

Better World / Autumn Kalquist—1st ed.

Printed in the United States of America

For Avalon.

CHAPTER ONE

C ontrol.

That's all Maeve wanted, but in the fleet, no one had that. Every day you woke sweating in a too-warm metal box, wondering if this was the day the fleet used you up for good. So after thinking about it long and hard, she'd come up with a solution. There was only one choice—one way to control her fate.

She had to kill herself.

Today was Maeve's eighteenth birthday, and what better day to end her life than on the day she'd come into it? A creak sounded, and Maeve jumped and took another furtive glance down the dark corridor. Here on the

London's sublevels, lume bars at half-power cast flickering light on dented metal walls and grease-stained floors. She let out a breath. Just the complaint of an ancient ship carrying them on their relentless journey through space. No one was down here—almost everyone should still be sleeping, and the first shift buzzer wouldn't sound for another half hour.

The power core made it so bloody hot, her skin was practically melting. She wiped her forehead and wiggled in her suit as sweat ran down her back. The stolen shift card bit into her palm, and a familiar wave of darkness swept over her, making it hard to breathe. She'd be in deep kak if they caught her here.

Too bad. Can't lash a dead person. She let out a laugh, and with new resolve, swiped the card across the panel. The door slid open in front of her, revealing the maintenance airlock beyond.

Her mirth faded as she entered. Red, blue, and green buttons lit up the control panel, and through the clear glasstex viewing pane, she could see the porthole in the airlock. Out there, a distant red planet spun in orbit, growing larger by the second. *Soren.*

Her heart jumped a little with that old hope, but it wasn't enough to overcome her despair.

There is no hope. Humanity had been searching for a new Earth for 300 years, and Soren was just another stop on the journey to extinction. Her parents had died too young getting here, and how many more lives would be lost once the fleet started mining that planet? Even if it had the metal they needed to build the next jump gate... the odds were against them. The next jump would just send the decaying fleet to another barren section of the galaxy.

This was the *end.* Humanity would die out, and their empty ships would drift forever through endless night. And who would be left to care?

Not me. Maeve swiped the card across the rusty scanner and activated the countdown sequence with a delay. Her heart sped up as she set the card down, so there could be no chance of changing her mind once she entered the airlock.

The warning alarm went off, and she hurried through the sliding door. It locked with a clack of finality behind her. Red lights flickered on and began blinking in time with the alarms. In sixty seconds, the airlock would open, and she'd be swept into space. No more darkness. Just a moment of pain, and then the blissful end.

Her fear and anticipation mounted with each cycle of the alarm. How much would it hurt? There were an infinite number of excruciating ways to die on this ship... and this was supposed to be the easiest way to go. Would it be?

She clenched and unclenched her fists and stared out the porthole, at the red planet ahead, trying to clear her mind of everything. But fear and doubt grew within her, making her shake.

Amazing how long a minute felt when you knew it was your last.

Come on.

Any second now.

The red lights abruptly shut off, and Maeve whirled, her blood pumping even harder as she sought out the intruder on the other side of the glass. Fierce anger rushed through her that she'd lost control *again*, but her rage fled when she glimpsed his face.

The blood drained from her cheeks when they made eye contact, and her determination to die wavered.

Dritan Corinth.

Brown skin, handsome features, his expression a mask to conceal his feelings. But the betrayal in his intense hazel eyes gave him away. She dropped her gaze to the scuffed metal floor, focusing on the line of rivets down the center of it as the door slid open.

"Maeve." Dritan walked over and grabbed her hand, swallowing her small one in his. The touch made her flinch, and her eyes burned as she finally looked up. Her choice had clearly hurt him, but her blood still churned with anger that he'd stopped her.

"Come to wish me a Lucky Birthday?" she asked brightly, ripping her hand away.

He narrowed his eyes at her and pushed a strand of her short black hair off her face. "I had to hack the panel to follow you in here," he said, his voice tight. He held up their enforcer's card, retrieved from the control room. "Fenton's?"

"Yeah. Fenton's. Should learn to guard his pockets better."

She'd waited until their new enforcer had been stumbling back to his bunk with the others, all of them stupid off bootleg. Then she'd plucked the card right from his pocket. It was the *bravest* thing she'd ever done.

Ironic, considering only cowards airlocked themselves, robbing the fleet of a colonist who could work. But fuck the fleet. It'd robbed *her* of her parents. And so many people she'd known, dead too soon. Now that she'd lost the last thing she cared about, there was really no reason to continue suffering, trying to live with the dark pain every damn day. Maeve cast a longing glance through the porthole, at the red planet in the distance. She should be out *there* right now.

"We   gotta   go," Dritan said roughly.

Maeve slammed her fists into his chest, shoving him off-balance. "You can go. I'm staying right here."

A flash of anger lit up Dritan's face as he grabbed her arm. "We'll talk about this out there."

Maeve's eyes burned as he half-dragged her out of the airlock, through the control room, and back out into the corridor.

The panel was off out there, wires ripped apart and twisted together. Dritan had risked *everything* hacking in. Messing with card access was practically treason, though they wouldn't kill him if they found out. They'd just lash him hard enough he wouldn't walk straight for a week.

She stood beside him, arms crossed over her chest as he squinted in the dim light, unwinding wires and returning everything to its former state. Maeve shook her head. He was too smart, meddling with hardware that shouldn't be hackable, fixing it all, even when none of the right parts were available.

After replacing the panel, he turned to face her—towering above her, like everyone did.

That, along with the way he stared her down, made her feel like a kid in caretaker sector again.

"Don't look at me like that." Her chest tightened as she forced herself to hold his accusatory gaze.

He grabbed her by the shoulders, gently, and stooped so he was at eye level with her. "I won't ask *why*. I don't have to... I get it. But at least tell me this... Is it out of your system now?"

"I dunno." Maeve shrugged. "Am I still here?"

"Dammit, M!" He squeezed her shoulders and let go, running a hand through his short curls, pulling on them. "We can't be down here right now. We'll get back to singles sector before the buzzer and drop the card outside Fenton's bunk. He'll think he just lost it."

He took a deep breath and nodded to himself. "Then everything will be *fine*."

Oh, Dritan. Always expecting the best, even when every possible outcome was awful. Not that Maeve had the heart to remind him of that.

Dritan gave her one last veiled look, then pocketed Fenton's card and gestured for her to walk. She whirled and strode down the corridor, her heart pounding as each step took her farther from her planned escape.

At least Dritan had shut up. Others would have judged and turned her in to the enforcers. But Dritan wasn't like that.... He never wanted to shame anyone. Since the day he'd arrived on this ship, an unwanted orphan, he'd *always* had her back. Yet she hadn't given him a single thought tonight. Guilt niggled at her, but she pushed it away.

They reached the stairwell and ascended the worn metal stairs, leaving the deep hum of the power core behind. Fresh air cooled Maeve's overheated skin, and the temperature continued to drop the deeper they went into singles sector. As they hurried past dozens of doors, all she heard was the creaking of the ship and the ceaseless whirring of the air re-cyc fans.

Their boots sank into the foam flooring with every step, masking their passage. The newness of it contrasted sharply with the old metal walls. Those were scuffed, dented, even rusted in places, despite the fact that the *London* manufactured all the fleet's sheet metal. Kind of hard to make enough metal to replace what needed replacing when the only metal they'd seen in two decades came from asteroids.

A toilet flushed in the shared lav to their right, and Dritan quickened his pace. He put a hand on Maeve's shoulder, urging her onward. The deka was waking up. Soon the first shift buzzer would go off, and all the unpaired workers would flow from their cubics for first mess.

The unpaired enforcers were at the back of the sector, with the best and biggest rooms and the most comfortable bunks, or so Maeve had heard. Not that any of them appreciated their luck. She flared her nostrils and ripped the card from Dritan's grasp to drop it outside Fenton's door.

As they turned to go, Maeve heard the awful whisper of a well-oiled door sliding open.

"What the fuck you two doing here?" a voice slurred.

They whirled to find Fenton standing there, and Maeve's chest seized with fear. It took all she had not to look at the card where it lay mere inches from his boots.

Fenton glared at them with puffy blue eyes in that squinty, suspicious way of his, his mussed red hair sticking up. His gaze flicked from Dritan to Maeve. And it slid down her face and body, lingering on the slight curves visible through her suit. Her skin crawled at the way he was looking at her. Like he was starving, and she was galley grub.

"*Why* are you here?" he said, drawing the words out.

Dritan looked like he was getting ready to lie, but Fenton hated Dritan even worse than Maeve. Better for her to take the blame.

"I had to take a kak," she said. "Our lav had a line. Yours didn't. When ya gotta go, ya gotta go."

Fenton's mouth twisted with disgust. "Sub halfs don't get to kak in enforcer lavs. Do it again, you'll get a demerit."

"Yes, Sir."

Dritan pressed his lips together, amusement in his eyes.

Fenton noticed. "And you, Corinth. What'd I tell you? You don't fix that uniform, it'll be another demerit and reduced rations."

Dritan's green suit was as tattered and grease-stained as Maeve's. No help for it when the *Vancouver*, their textile ship, was overloaded with orders. But Fenton had hated Dritan since caretaker—since a day years ago when Fenton had tried to bully Maeve, and Dritan had stopped him. Having *him* as their new enforcer was bad news.

"Yes, Sir," Dritan said. "I'll clean and patch it again tonight."

"Good. Now get lost."

Maeve and Dritan didn't need to be told twice. They turned and left, walking as fast as they could.

Once they were out of sight, Maeve nudged Dritan. "When he finds that card, he'll know—"

"He won't know," Dritan said in a near-whisper. "He can suspect all he wants, but he can't prove anything. And if they do notice it got used, they'll blame *him*. He can't admit he lost it."

"You know..." Maeve rubbed her stomach, groaning in fake pain. "I have the *strangest* urge to take a kak in an enforcer lav right now."

Dritan suppressed a grin and shook his head.

"We only allow enforcer asses on our seats," Maeve slurred. "Take a kak again—face a demerit."

They both laughed, and the earlier tension between them vanished. The buzzer went off, and halfs began flowing out of their cubics— a sea of mostly sublevel workers in green suits mingled with techs wearing black. Most were apprentices, ages twelve to eighteen, but a few older faces joined the rush, halfs like Maeve—between eighteen and twenty-one— who were late to pair. The unwelcome thought of pairing, having to choose a husband, made Maeve's stomach turn.

"I heard the rationing will be over soon," Dritan said. "The *Meso* may have fixed their root rot problem."

"Wouldn't bet on it. We should hurry before the cooks run out."

As they headed for the stairs, a dozen enforcers in navy suits arrived, and everyone jumped out of the way to let them through. Fenton was among them, and he shot Dritan and Maeve a dirty look as he pushed past.

Enforcers always acted like they deserved to live and eat up on executive level. But only the head enforcer got to do *that*, and only colonists born on exec-level could get the job. Fenton and his like were just glorified sub workers with inflated heads. All you needed to do was get the right people to favor you, or like in Fenton's case, be born to enforcer parents.

For Maeve and Dritan, sub parents meant a sub's life. Just about every one of them would die early from some terrible accident or accelerated power core sickness. *Any* control the colonists thought they had over their lives was an illusion.

A mistake of birth decided your entire life on this damn ship.

Maeve's despair crept back—a cruel nothingness that sapped her energy and dulled every sensation.

When they finally reached the stairs, Dritan wrapped an arm around her, and her throat closed at the feeling of his strong arm on her back.

"Things will get better," he said low in her ear. "I promise. They will."

He released her, and she gave him a small smile, nodding like she believed him. The look of relief on his face was worth the lie.

But was she *glad* he'd stopped her from airlocking herself?

No.

If he'd come for her a few seconds later, she'd be done with all this, floating free in open space. Darkness churned within her, death still beckoning.

And when death called, it always got an answer.

CHAPTER TWO

"*S*oren."
"*First landfall.*"

The words were on everyone's lips as Maeve and Dritan headed for first mess. The undercurrent of excitement in the stairwell and galley were palpable—a nervous energy flooding the deka and putting her on edge.

The main galley was an enormous open space with long metal tables and enough benches to seat thousands. The level filled up fast, dividing into the usual groups. Nearly six hundred techs sat at their tables at the far end, and more than twenty-five hundred subs sat at the other. The enforcers numbered two hundred and fifty and usually sat at the two long tables between the techs and the subs—

not important enough to get tech work, but too good to mingle with the subs they oversaw.

In the far corner of the sub section, the maimed and useless gathered. The Outcast. Missing limbs, ill health, twisted minds. Unable to really do their duties, yet still using fleet resources. If *they* airlocked themselves, no one would care or complain.

The cooks had already started plating the hot quin, and the smell made Maeve's mouth water. She and Dritan got in line, but as they did, she accidentally bumped into a sub in front of her.

The half she'd touched whirled around. It was a blond sub half named Bea—they'd known her in caretaker.

"Watch yourself." Bea wrinkled her nose.

Maeve held up a hand of apology, and the girl turned back to talk to her friends.

As the line moved, Bea's next words filtered back to them. "...still unpaired. Deevy glitch."

Maeve's nostrils flared at the insult, and she balled her hands into fists. Dritan grabbed her wrist swiftly, giving the barest shake of his head.

He was right. Bea wasn't worth it.

Face flaming, Maeve aggressively grabbed a full tray from the line and stalked toward their usual table. Fucking glitches. Who were they to call her a deviant? They knew nothing. Population Management regulations gave her until age twenty-one to pair. And if she didn't make a choice by then... they'd choose for her.

She slid down on the bench at her crew's table and tried to throttle her anger by shoving the bland quin grain down her throat. Dritan didn't say another word, thank Infinitek. If she could *just* get through today without snapping, she'd spend tonight coming up with a new plan of escape. And next time, she'd do it right—she wouldn't get caught.

A few minutes later, the rest of the crew showed up at the table. Quiet Hyun and her husband Vinay sat across from them. The new crew leader, Kevan, smacked Dritan on the back in a friendly hello as he settled on the other side of him.

Gilly bounded over last with a full tray and the sort of energy only a new half could have. She grinned as she slid onto the bench beside Maeve. "Morning!"

Maeve gave her a weak smile and turned away. The kid had been following her around since they'd put her on the crew a month ago. At twelve, she was their youngest member, and she sure acted it.

"They're briefing us about the planet to-day," Kevan said matter-of-factly.

Hyun gave them all a small smile. "A tech told me they sent the probes ahead already. They got some data before they lost contact, so I guess we'll be making first landfall soon."

"Only three transports get to go this time," Vinay said around a mouthful of food. "Might be the *London* won't supply workers for the first round."

The crew had talked about this at almost every meal for months now. Just the same stupid speculation, over and over.

Maeve knew she should stay quiet, but the words fell out of her mouth anyway. "Give it up already. We make *metal*. Get it? Who do you think they'll send? Colonists from the *Meso*? They're not tryin'a grow quin down there."

Everyone looked surprised at her words, except oblivious Gilly.

"I'd go if they chose me," she piped up. "Can you imagine? Getting to be the first one to set foot on a new planet...?" She turned to Maeve, her eyes wide. "Oh! This *is* a lucky birthday for you. Aren't you eighteen today?"

"Ah, yes. *So* lucky." Maeve's voice dripped with sarcasm, and she added in a quiet voice, "Here comes the death draft."

Kevan snorted, and the rest of them stared at her like she'd grown an extra limb. Dritan elbowed her lightly in the ribs, and she shoved more food into her mouth. It suddenly tasted like dust.

All the colonists who mined the last planet were long dead, but everyone alive had heard the rumors. It was said that the colonists who made first landfall on a new planet always died a horrible death.

Every. Single. Time.

There were a million calculations to get right for a first landing, so it wasn't surprising that the ancient transports crashed or got destroyed trying to descend through the atmosphere. But it had to be done. The fleet needed the data the first transports would capture to ensure the second wave made it down.

Dritan cleared his throat, breaking the awkward silence, and winked at Gilly. "You're right. We'd be lucky to get the chance. Maybe we'll get to if we reach another planet after *we're* eighteen."

Maeve kept her mouth shut this time. Did Dritan really believe his own kak?

Gilly perked up. "You know, my mama told me this planet could have what we need to build the next jump gate. New Earth could be *one* jump away."

She'd finally brought up the hope no one else ever dared voice. They all hesitated, and then Kevan grinned at the new half.

"I hope I'm around to see it," he said.

"Me, too," Vinay and Hyun said at the same time. They exchanged the kind of look only a paired couple could exchange, full of unspoken thoughts and nauseating affection. Hyun cuddled closer to Vinay as they finished their food, and he wrapped an arm around her.

Maeve's heart twisted just from watching the display. She sucked down her water and nearly spat it back out in disgust. Musty with a hint of metal. Bottom of the tank, definitely. Was the *Oslo* running low yet again?

Gilly dropped her fork to her plate and pointed toward the double doors. "Look!"

As the rest of the galley became aware of who was walking through the doors, the din reached new heights, everyone talking at once, getting to their feet in a rush.

Execs.

Captain Kerrigan walked in first, stocky and ruddy-faced, with his head of red hair. Lead Tech Miller followed, and behind them was Head Enforcer Jacobs. The three of them went to the back of the galley to a raised dais and screen where news and schedules were usually displayed.

Maeve's pulse picked up, and bitter saliva flooded her mouth. She swallowed it back, trying to keep the disgust off her face as the head enforcer took the stage beside the others. Jacobs was tall, strong, with the kind of average good looks that inspired trust. But she was a *traitor* to the subs she was supposed to oversee.

Two months ago, there had been a fire in the sector where they manufactured hull panels. Jacobs had given the order to vent all the oxygen without even trying to fight it with extinguishers first. Twenty subs had died that shift, including *both* of Maeve's parents. They'd only been thirty-four years old.

Maeve fought to keep the hate off her face as the head enforcer lifted the amplifier to her mouth.

Her voice came through the small black box with a crackle. "Good morning, colonists of the *London*. Please take your seats."

Everyone settled back down on the benches, and the energy in the air infected even Maeve, her stomach fluttering sickly with it.

Jacobs gave the captain the amplifier, and the room quieted in expectation.   Gilly was breathing fast, and her eyes were glassy, riveted to the execs. A little twinge of guilt hit Maeve over the way she'd acted, so she patted Gilly's hand to try to calm her down. Gilly grabbed Maeve's hand in a death grip.

"This is a day that will be remembered," the Captain said. "The *London* slowed to a complete stop half an hour ago. I'm proud to announce that we have finally reached *Soren*, named so in honor of our leader and her family's long service to this fleet. President Sorenson briefed all the deka captains earlier from the bridge of the flagship *Paragon*. She has high hopes for our upcoming mission."

Excited murmurs rose in the crowd, and Gilly squeezed Maeve's hand so hard Maeve thought she heard bones crunching.

The Captain held up a hand for silence, and the murmuring faded. "The last planet we found in this system had resources, but none of the martisium we need to build the next jumpgate. Soren is another chance for us all. The first step is landfall and testing the soil.

Out of the ten dekas, three will supply transports for the first landing. The *Perth*, the *Kyoto*, and the *London*."

The mining ship, the power ship, and the metal-working ship. All the dekas that made the raw materials for the jumpgate. A flicker of fear raced through Maeve, and by the surge of noise in the room, everyone else was experiencing the same.

"We've been training our landfall flight crew for over a year now, and it is an *honor* to be chosen for this," the captain continued, "but as most of you know, it is customary for seven additional crew members to help man the transports. Our workers will be essential to helping the *Perth* search for and identify available resources on the planet. Today, we will hold a lottery for the seven. Only our best *unpaired* techs and sublevel workers over the age of eighteen will be entered."

Hyun and Vinay looked at each other with relief, and the tension in the rest of the galley instantly went down a step as every couple realized they wouldn't be in the first landfall lottery.

Fucking wonderful. Maeve exchanged a glance with Kevan, who had gone pale. He was almost forty-five, older than most, but since his wife had died in an accident years ago, he'd also be a candidate.

The captain held up a hand, and the galley quieted once more. "If you are over the age of eighteen and would like to volunteer ahead of the draft, raise your hand now."

The room went utterly silent as each colonist cast sidelong glances at friends and enemies to see if anyone would volunteer now that the possibility of a *jump gate* had arrived.

Maeve stared down at her tray, shoulders tight. Did the captain think they were all idiots? The execs would never send *their* unpaired down there to die some terrible death.

If one person had volunteered, maybe more would have. But not a single hand went up. When it was clear no one would volunteer, the captain spoke. "Then I wish each of you the best of luck. While some must make first landfall, the rest of us have to stay focused on our duties. Our jobs are now more important than ever. May Soren be even richer than Farragut was."

Maeve's whole crew looked hopeful at the words, eyes shining like Gilly's.

"A better world awaits," the captain said, his voice strong.

"A better world awaits," the crowd intoned.

Maeve mouthed the words but felt none of the raw hope on the faces around her.

The head enforcer took the amplifier back. "I will be choosing only a few of our best workers. If you've shown a strong commitment to duty and excellence on the job, you have a chance to be one of the chosen. Good luck to you all."

The Lead Tech took the amplifier next, turning to address his techs in their corner. "I've compiled a list of my best techs for the job. If you have experience working with the metal analysis software, you're at the top of the list. I wish you all luck as well."

With that, the three of them strode back out of the galley. The minute the doors slid shut behind them, the low conversation escalated to a roar. Dritan   stayed silent, flashing a look at Maeve, noting the way Gilly was still hanging onto her hand. Maeve tried to wiggle out of her sweaty grasp, and Gilly's cheeks went flame red as she dropped Maeve's hand.

"I bet they'll choose you, Maeve." Gilly said in a rush. "You had one of the highest scores of anyone, didn't you? Our caretaker told us that."

Now the whole crew and even some subs further down the table were looking in her direction. Maeve shrugged and grabbed her tray off the table. "Nope. Must have me mixed up with someone else. If they're choosing the best, that counts me out."

Dritan raised a brow at her, but everyone's focus shifted to the screen above the dais as the shift schedule came up. Maeve didn't wait around to see where she had to risk her life today.

She returned her tray to the front and headed for the doors. Gilly was right. Maeve *had* gotten one of the highest scores. In fact, the only person in recent memory to get a higher score on the hardware exams was Dritan. And he damn well knew that.

He caught up to her as she reached the stairwell. "We're on P4 today," he said, out of breath. "Looks like they're opening up the jumpgate sector, and we're one of the crews going in."

Maeve's mouth went dry. The components in there were *old*. And old meant dangerous in this fleet. "That's great."

She started down the stairs, and Dritan quickened his pace to keep up with her. "Gilly looks up to you, you know."

"Yeah, well I don't need any of that."

"A good sub, like *you*, could teach her a lot—"

"Experience in the sublevels will do that just fine." She picked up her pace, navigating the flow of people moving in both directions.

"If you just spent some time with her, maybe—"

"Drop it." How could he expect her to mentor a half when she believed in duty so little she'd tried to airlock herself last shift?

"Wait."

Maeve ignored him and pushed ahead through the P4 doors. The heat of the power core rushed over her, sweat instantly popping up on her forehead, and the core filled her up with its vibration, its ceaseless hum.

"Maeve." Dritan grabbed her by the arm and pulled her to the side of the corridor, forcing her to look up at him.

"What?"

"We're *so close*." He sounded vulnerable, but there was a strength in his tone, the hope she couldn't feel.

"What if we're not?"

Dritan's brow furrowed, like he couldn't believe she'd really said it. It was a question she'd always kept to herself, but she couldn't take it back now.

"What if there *is* no better world?" she said, too loudly. "What if we're really cursed to wander the stars for an eternity for what we did to Earth?"

Dritan recovered from his surprise, tightening his jaw as he glanced at some subs pushing past. "Our ancestors did that. Not us," he said, keeping his voice low. "And if you really believed that, then you'd believe the rest. The stories say if we all do our duty to the fleet to ensure humanity's survival, we'll be forgiven for what we did. Which means we *will* find our new world."

Maeve rolled her eyes. "Well, I *don't* believe that. And you don't either."

"Maybe not, but I know we'll eventually find a new home. Maybe not in our lifetime, but... someday. We just need to keep searching." His voice took on an edge, a telltale sign his passionate streak was about to overtake his ability to reason logically. "If we *are* meant to wander, we should go out fighting. Because you know what? If we can't even fight for our own survival, then the old stories were right. We wouldn't deserve a better world. We need to stay clear-headed and determined and get the job done. Not just *quit* before we get there."

Like I tried to quit.

His eyes widened as he realized what he'd implied. "I didn't mean you. I meant—"

"Doesn't matter." Maeve said simply, and then walked toward the cold jumpgate sector.

She'd held the same hopes as him when she was younger, but they were gone now, and she wasn't the only person who eventually doubted the idea of a new Earth. Colonists quit every year, most of them airlocking themselves. It was usually the Outcast and those dying of core sickness who did it... but not always.

Dritan was wrong. He was brave and passionate about doing his duty, but *wrong*. She'd never shared her doubts with him before this, because he didn't question things. Ever. He just accepted them. Sometimes she wished she could be more like him, content and optimistic about the future... then the darkness would stay away.

What if quitting *was* the only escape?

CHAPTER THREE

Four crews gathered outside the jumpgate sector, including Maeve and Dritan's. All around Maeve, subs performed their good luck rituals. One man lifted his sleeve and kissed the infinity symbol tattooed there. A woman checked the pockets on her suit one by one, ensuring they were all zippered or buttoned shut. Next to Maeve, a half was tying her boot laces in complex knots, then tucking them in carefully.

Maeve resisted the urge to smooth her collar and cup a hand over the star-shaped pendant in her pocket. Her mother had been wearing the star for luck when she died. But it hadn't helped her then, had it?

Everyone stood at attention as the head enforcer arrived, Fenton and three other enforcers trailing her. Another spike of hate seared through Maeve at the sight of them, but she pushed it down and focused on what they were about to do. How many times had she walked past this door, wondering what lay on the other side?

Jacobs swept her card across the scanner, and the doors creaked open slowly, whining on ancient bearings.

Maeve barely breathed as she followed everyone into the sector. High ceilings rose over row upon row of strange-yet-familiar machinery. Everything was built with interchangeable parts in the fleet, but this set-up was different. These were *old* machines, rusted and dented, extending from floor to ceiling. Assembly belts wound through the sector, and enormous curved metal tubes ran above them, parallel with the floor. Ladders led to catwalks providing access to every tall machine and pipe.

Jacobs took the enforcers aside to give them their orders, and the crews stood by—every sub talking in low tones. Maeve stayed quiet and pretended not to notice when Gilly grabbed her sleeve and tugged.

The jumpgate sector. Maeve's heart beat faster just looking at it all. If Soren had martisium, they'd build each piece of the gate from the precious metal *here,* in this room. Once assembled in space, the massive circle would draw power from every ship, and the system's sun if necessary, to create a wormhole that would take the fleet to a new part of the galaxy.

Maeve might not be a tech, but she had enough math to know the odds of the next jump leading to a habitable planet were slim. Once they jumped, they'd just travel for decades until they found the next planet with resources to build another gate. Unless the ships fell apart first... and they probably would. *That's why none of this matters.*

Fenton walked over to their crew, looking as constipated as always. "Crew 104, this way."

They followed him deep into the sector, to a far wall next to one of the enormous tubes.

Beneath it, stood a massive metal box where the control panel was located.

Fenton leaned against the wall, arms crossed over his chest. "Each crew will be working on one of the gate presses. Head Enforcer Jacobs wants 'em up and running by midbreak. This is yours. Now get to work."

Kevan frowned, surveying the press, then looked at his crew. "Bound to be some glitches in this sector. Been cold for decades. Vinay, Hyun, help me get the panels off the control box. Maeve, Dritan, check to see if we got any manuals inside the press."

Gilly trailed after Maeve and Dritan as they peered into the opening of the curved pipe. Pipes were the worst. This one looked like all the others, except for the thick curved rod running down the center of it. The rod was covered in an uneven, jagged surface, and looked like it was meant to spin in place.

"Tight fit," Dritan said.

Maeve's heart leapt into her throat. "I'll go."

Dritan grabbed a helio from the workcase and tossed it to her. She tapped the cool metal sphere, and it rose in the air, hovering beside her shoulder. The small globe lit up like a tiny sun to light her way.

Dritan gave Maeve a knee up, and she crawled into the dark pipe. It was stifling in here, and sweat dripped into her eyes and soaked through her suit.

So. Tight. She squeezed between the center rod and the side of the tube and tried to keep her breathing even. A few feet in, the helio lit up a labeled panel.

As she twisted to face it, the jagged edges on the rod jabbed through her suit. She lifted up the panel and squinted to assess its condition. The wires and components looked a bit brittle, but they might work.

"Found it." Her voice echoed down the pipe. "Got a panel in here. Manual restart."

Maeve's relief grew with every inch of progress she made toward the exit, and then she dropped back to the floor. Out there, Gilly was talking loudly.

"So what does *this* section do when we make the jumpgate?" she asked Fenton, voice full of wonder.

Everyone was staring at her, then at Fenton, who looked like he'd just eaten a rotten bite of quin. "You call me *Enforcer Fenton*, half. This section makes a part of the jump gate."

Gilly's forehead wrinkled with confusion. "I know *that*, Enforcer Fenton, but *which* part?"

Maeve wanted to slap a hand across Gilly's mouth to shut her up. Fenton acted like every question was a challenge, and they needed him to go *away* and sneak hooch like usual, not hover around mucking things up.

"But how does the gate work, Sir?" Gilly ran a hand down the panel and looked at the grime it had left on her palm.

Couldn't she tell how tense her line of questioning was making the whole crew?

Fenton grasped the stunner looped through his belt and shot Gilly a dark look. "We need to work, *half*. Not ask stupid questions."

"Let's try starting it," Kevan said quickly.

They all stepped back as he tried flipping the switch.

Nothing happened even after several tries, as expected. Kevan dragged the workcase over to the panel and started assessing the components. Fenton asked for a report, and Kevan explained the sorry state of the control panel.

Gilly frowned. "How are we supposed to know how to fix this when our enforcer doesn't even know what it does?"

"Shh." Maeve lifted her brows meaningfully. "The components are all interchangeable... even here. We can get it online, even if *he* can't."

Gilly let out a giggle, and Dritan leaned closer to them both. "I think this is where they shape the metal," he said kindly, pointing at the press. "The whole process probably starts at that holding tank we saw near the entrance. That's where the metal will be forged before we shape it."

Fenton and Kevan had finished their conversation and caught the tail-end of Dritan's explanation. Fenton's expression soured, and his eyes took on a nasty glint.

He detached a helio from his workbelt and tossed it to Dritan. "You get to start on this panel, Corinth. *Alone.* You can fix it, can't ya?"

"Yes, sir." Dritan took the helio to the panel, and Kevan stepped back, looking grim. Fenton leaned against the nearest wall, a smirk on his face, watching Dritan intently.

Maeve tried to keep her expression neutral as she moved closer to watch Dritan work, but inside she was seething. Assigning jobs was Kevan's duty, not Fenton's, but Kevan wouldn't go against an enforcer's orders, and no one would risk reporting Fenton. You got one enforcer in trouble, the rest of them would make sure you paid for it.

The control components looked positively ancient, unreliable. *Dangerous.* They should be handling this as a *team.*

Dritan opened the workcase, exposing the motley assortment of tools and plastic, metal, and wire components. He assessed the components in the panel, looking for the main power source and for any burnt out sections. When he located the source, he ripped a few wires out and replaced them with newer ones from the case.

The low hum of the power core ran through Maeve as she watched, and voices drifted across the space from where other crews worked. But otherwise, the dead machines made it eerily silent.

After a few tense minutes, Dritan strode over to the switch and hit it.

The press shuddered to life, and Maeve jumped at the sound and the vibrations beneath her boots. The press's inner walls expanded and contracted as the center rod rotated. Pride surged through her at Dritan's success. That'd show Fenton.

But Dritan looked worried for some reason, and then the gears ground to a screeching halt, the whole tube shuddering. He quickly flipped the switch and went back to the panel.

Concentrating, he gingerly touched the components, nodded to himself, and bent to change out one of the wires.

When he pulled it out, sparks flew. Dritan flew backward and slammed into the wall.

Maeve's heart seemed to stop beating as she ran to his unmoving body. *Don't be dead. Please don't be dead.*

He wouldn't be the first sub to be electrocuted by faulty components. In her peripheral vision, Fenton yelled something to Vinay. The panel had caught fire, and flames leapt high as they scrambled to get an extinguisher on it. Biting smoke filled her nostrils and stung her eyes, but she couldn't focus on anything but Dritan.

She knelt beside him and gently squeezed his arm, nearly crying with relief when his eyes opened. He looked dazed but otherwise uninjured.

Alive. "You and your damn lucky genes," Maeve murmured.

Dritan cracked a pained smile. "I'd hardly call that lucky. Fuck! That hurt."

She lightly smacked his arm. "You've survived kak that'd kill another sub. Yeah, I call it lucky."

Hyun shook her head at Maeve as she helped Dritan to his feet. "Lucky genes."

"I told him," Maeve said.

Everyone said it. He'd been shuffled from ship to ship as a child—no couple wanted an orphan if it meant losing their spot in the Population lottery. But that's where his ill luck ended. This wasn't his first near miss with faulty machinery. He'd had deep wounds that barely missed vital organs, and before he'd been placed on Maeve's crew, there'd been hull breaches and fatal accidents that happened on jobs he'd just been rotated from... Kak, he even won most games of chips.

Maeve helped Dritan stand, holding his arm tight so he could lean on her.

The rest of the crew was checking the damage to the components, but Fenton was watching Maeve help Dritan with an odd expression on his face. It made her skin prickle the same way it always did, and she let go of Dritan's arm. Fucking Fenton. His insistence that Dritan work alone could have gotten him *killed*.

"Gotta replace all of this now," Kevan said from the panel.

"Head enforcer wants it *working*." Fenton said sharply. "Use the manual restart."

Kevan shook his head. "Sir, I think... I *know* we can fix this from out here. Might be we didn't get the press offline in time. It could still be live when we get it working. It's not safe in there."

Fenton's face reddened. "You questioning my orders, Sarkis?"

Kevan narrowed his eyes like he wanted to do just that, but when Fenton tapped his finger against his electric baton in open threat, Kevan stepped back, raising both hands.

"No, Sir. I'm not questioning your orders."

"Someone's going in there and fixing this. Now."

"Yes, Sir."

They all glanced back into the press. The inner walls of the pipe had narrowed further, even closer to the rod than before, leaving hardly any space. None of them would fit through there. Well, no one except Maeve. Or Gilly, who was even smaller. But they wouldn't send a new half to do this job. She didn't have the training yet.

Adrenaline coursed through Maeve's veins as she realized what that meant, and she looked toward the outer doors, contemplating running. She wasn't gonna die like this. That thing would eat her alive if it turned on with her inside it. Dritan exchanged a worried glance with Maeve, obviously thinking the same thing.

Then everyone was looking at her, and her shoulders slumped.

"One of us has to go in there," Kevan said. "And—"

"I'll do it," Dritan said. "I think I can squeeze in there."

Fenton let out a harsh laugh. "So you can fuck it up again? You won't fit in there. Nah." He sniffed, and his creepy gaze fell on Maeve. "Vasquez. You."

They all looked at her, and her heart pounded so fast she forgot to breathe. Every cell in her body screamed at her, told her if she went in that tube she'd never come out alive. But she couldn't get her legs to move, couldn't find the strength to run.

Bile rose in her throat as she met Fenton's hard eyes. "No."

Gilly audibly gasped, and the rest of them went still.

Fenton's brows went up. "That was an order."

"No." Maeve said it more forcefully. "You want it restarted? Do it yourself."

Fenton's eyes took on the gleam they always did when he got a chance to lash one of them. She clenched her hands into fists and prepared to fight back.

His mouth twisted cruelly as he removed his stunner and extended the baton, activating it. Blue light crackled along its length, and Maeve's brain begged her to get away. But her legs were rooted in place.

"Ten lashes for that. On your knees."

"You first."

His eyes lit up, and he lunged for her, violently shoving her sideways so his baton connected with the back of her knees.

The shock of electricity made every muscle in Maeve's body seize, stealing her control. She sank to the floor, eyes watering, trying to suck oxygen into her lungs.

Fenton put even more force behind the next hit. The metal rod slammed across her back, the current paralyzing her muscles again. Maeve stayed with the pain, not trying to escape it. *Just breathe in between the strikes.*

Another lash. Then another. They seemed to go on forever, but when Maeve counted ten, Fenton stopped.

"You ready to work, Vasquez?" Fenton was breathing hard, and he pulled her around, forced her to look up at him.

Her raw back screamed at the movement, and she glared up at him, her hate even stronger than the pain. "Fuck. You."

"Ten more for that." He kicked her down so he could strike her back again.

Her heart beat an erratic rhythm, threatening to explode.

Each strike was worse than the last. Every time her muscles stopped seizing, she tried to suck air in and failed before the next strike fell. Black swam around the edges of her vision. *I'm going to suffocate.*

But she didn't. Somehow she held onto consciousness, and at twenty, he stopped.

Wetness trickled down Maeve's back, stinging like fire along her wounds. She panted hard, sucking in gulps of air, her heart thumping wildly.

Dritan came to help her up, and Maeve kept her eyes on him, unable to look at anyone else.

"In the tube, Vasquez."

Maeve met Fenton's eyes and let her hate show, determined to refuse until he threw her in the brig. Nothing he could do would break her, not now.

He couldn't break her when she was already broken.

"I'm small enough," Gilly said. Her face was pale, and she gave Maeve a concerned look before grabbing a helio from the air. "I can do this."

"No!" Maeve pushed Dritan away. "I'll go. I'll go." Maeve said it without thinking, but the second she did, she realized her mistake.

Fenton smiled like he'd won something. "The *coward* can sit this one out. I have a volunteer. We don't turn down volunteers."

Dritan squeezed Maeve's arm and gave her a warning look.

Kevan walked with Gilly to the tube. "I'll talk you through it."

He helped Gilly climb up, and Maeve tried to ignore the stinging flesh on her back as she stumbled over to the switch, ready to hit it at the first sign of trouble.

Gilly crawled into the narrow tube, the helio lighting the inside so they could see her progress. When she reached the panel and popped it off, Kevan guided her, telling her what to look for, which switches to pull. When they didn't work, he told her how to find the right wires to adjust so the machine would start with a delay.

Maeve's pulse roared in her head, making her dizzy as Gilly finished the job.

"I think I did it!" Gilly's proud voice echoed down the tube.

Maeve breathed again as Gilly crawled toward the exit, and the rest of the crew seemed to sigh with the same shared relief.

Gilly was nearly to the end when the machine groaned to life. Time stopped. The grind of each gear reverberated through Maeve's skull, and the ground shuddered in slow motion beneath her boots.

No! Her hand slammed down on the switch. *Please don't be too late.*

The walls constricted inside the pipe, trapping Gilly's tiny body between them and the rotating center rod. Her screams pierced the air as her arm caught on the rod, rotating with it. Blood spattered the inside of the tube, and Gilly's screams got louder, and more and more desperate.

The scene before Maeve seemed filtered through smoke, everything disjointed, voices disconnected from moving bodies.

Dritan and Kevan dragging Gilly the rest of the way out of the pipe.

Vinay disappearing with a single word. "Medics."

Slick red blood dripped from the rod and formed a rivulet down the center of the pipe. Maeve swayed to the side, leaning against the wall as she watched drops of blood fall to the floor. She fought the urge to puke.

Everything abruptly sped up again to normal time, and her eyes jumped from person to person. Hyun had the emergency medkit open, and red still spurted from Gilly's clawed-up arm. Her hand was mangled beyond recognition, her arm twisted unnaturally. As Hyun shot her up with painmod, her small face went slack, mouth open, tears still trailing down her cheeks. Tiny drops fell to the floor, mingling with the blood there.

And instead of going to her, Maeve turned her head and refused to look.

Coward.

Fenton emerged in Maeve's line of sight, and she threw up her arms to protect her face just as his fist slammed into her.

He shoved Maeve into the wall, eyes blazing. "This is your fuckin' fault, Deev," he hissed. "I'm not taking the blame for this. It should have been you."

Red swam before her, rage and grief mingling together as she lowered her arms and stared back defiantly.

"No," her voice nearly broke, and she put more force behind it. "*You* made a bad call.

Next time, listen to subs who actually know how to do the work." She couldn't believe the words coming out of her mouth, and Fenton clearly couldn't either.

He slammed her into the metal wall again, and the lashes on her back screamed. "You'll regret that."

The head enforcer showed up, and Fenton released Maeve to go report the accident.

Maeve's breath caught as the head enforcer moved out of the way to let the medics run past.

Cassia. Her deep blue eyes, high cheekbones, delicate chin... she looked out of place down here in the depths of the ship. Too beautiful for all the pain and suffering. She didn't belong here, and she never had.

Maeve's heart twisted, and she pressed herself against the wall, knowing she should go to Gilly but unable to face Cassia. Not here. Not now, like this. Cassia had told her in no uncertain terms that their friendship was *over*.

The medics worked quickly, binding Gilly's arm and lifting her thin body onto the stretcher.

Cassia swiped a strand of dark brown hair off her cheek, leaving a smear of blood behind, and directed her medics back up to the medbay. Maeve averted her eyes, heart pounding, guilt tearing through her as they hurried past.

If Maeve had been the one to go in the press, she'd be dead right now or close to. And it would have been an excruciatingly painful way to go.

Lucky. Maeve felt lucky, even as Gilly suffered.

Not lucky. She was a coward, like Fenton had said.

The blackness inside Maeve rose up, suffocating her. Fenton was right.

It should've been me.

CHAPTER FOUR

Gilly's work had gotten their press up and running again, and the crew spent the rest of the shift cleaning her sticky blood from the press and identifying components that needed replacing in the main control panel.

No one talked about what had happened, and Maeve ignored all Dritan's attempts to corner her in private. She just counted down the minutes until midbreak, knowing what she needed to do. Going to medbay meant possibly seeing Cassia again, but she *had* to see Gilly. She needed to face what she'd done.

When midbreak arrived, she shot out of the sector, leaving Dritan and the rest of them behind. As she hurried up the stairs, weaving past techs and subs on their way to midmess, she tried to work up her courage.

Cassia's father was lead medic, so she lived on exec level—so far above Maeve's station, it was a wonder they'd ever become friends. But they had, and for the past three years, they'd spent hours together during free time, meeting on Observation and finding private places where they could get drunk off bootleg and dream about what New Earth would look like.

But *those* days were over. Cassia had been quite clear on that. Infinitek willing, she'd be at the galley right now.

The medbay was a huge cubic with more than two dozen cots. They were packed full of subs, as usual, with injuries ranging from the mild to the possibly fatal. But Maeve didn't see Gilly anywhere. She stepped out of the way as a medic bustled past, and she found herself rooted in place, transfixed by the helix and triquetra patch on his sleeve.

She took a deep breath and forced herself to keep walking to the back of the cubic. Cassia was there, and Maeve's stupid heart started fluttering the second she caught sight of her standing behind the station. Maeve's nails bit into her palms, and she forced herself to continue on.

When Cassia finally looked up and saw Maeve, her full lips parted. "What's wrong?" She came around the desk abruptly, searching Maeve for injury. "What happened?"

Maeve's cheeks warmed. "Not me. Gilly, a half on my crew."

Cassia just stared at her, the things they'd said the last time a sharp and awful thing between them. "You shouldn't be here without a chit."

"Well I am." Maeve forced her voice to come out strong. "And I want to see Gilly."

Cassia hesitated, watching the medic closest to them as he prepped painmod. When he disappeared behind the curtain to treat his next patient, Cassia grabbed Maeve's sleeve and dragged her to the door behind the station.

As they slipped through, Maeve's stomach churned. The cubic back here was reserved for surgery—for the worst injuries. This didn't bode well, but what had she really expected? A series of curtains split up the room, and Cassia led her through the first one.

Gilly was lying there in a deep sleep, looking so damn small. Maeve went to examine her, pulling the sheet back lightly, and the room spun around her as her worst fears were confirmed. *Amputated.*

Gilly's right arm was gone up to her elbow.

"She lost a lot of blood," Cassia said. "We'll have to keep her for a while."

"Lucky her," Maeve said. "She won't have to deal with demented Fenton anymore."

Cassia lifted her brow. "You know... she's *lucky* to be alive."

"Yeah, so am I."

"What do you mean?"

Maeve met Cassia's eyes. "I mean Fenton told *me* to get in the press. And I told *him* to go fuck himself."

"You..." Cassia went pale. "You did *what? You* disobeyed an enforcer?"

"He's an idiot. So, yes."

"Did he..."

"Lash me? Yep. Then Gilly volunteered to do my job." A lump formed in Maeve's throat, and she gently touched Gilly's shoulder, unable to tear her gaze from where her hand should be.

Gilly had been so excited to do her duty, so hopeful about Soren. And now...

"I'll take good care of her," Cassia said softly. "You don't need to be here. I... Let me get you some cream for your back."

She left the curtained enclosure to cross the partition to the next cot. Maeve took one last look at Gilly, then pushed through the curtain to the other side.

"Sit," Cassia said. "This will help with the sting."

"I really gotta get to midmess."

"Let me treat you." Cassia's voice was rough, and she stepped closer and touched the zipper at the top of Maeve's suit. "Please."

Without thinking, Maeve placed her hand over Cassia's. Sparks leapt between them, and tension thrummed in the small space, as dangerous as a live wire. The intensity of it hadn't diminished, even if Cassia claimed their friendship was over.

Neither one of them breathed as Maeve lifted Cassia's hand and pushed up her sleeve, revealing the infinity symbol tattoo there.

Maeve had expected it, of course. She'd known it would be there, but actually seeing it was strange. Horrible. Her own wrist still had the teardrop shape denoting her half status, but Cassia was paired now, her infinity complete. The other half of the symbol was dark with the fresh ink of a new tattoo.

"So how's the paired life?" Maeve asked lightly. "Must be nice having a whole exec cubic to yourselves."

"Don't," Cassia whispered.

Maeve dropped Cassia's wrist and turned away. She unzipped her suit in a fluid motion and shrugged it off her shoulders so it hung around her waist. The cool air of the medbay sent a shiver through her, and she crossed her arms over her bare breasts.

Cassia sucked in a breath. "Damn. He got you good."

Maeve was afraid her voice would betray her if she tried to answer, so she waited in silence, staring at a scuffed panel as Cassia collected her supplies.

Her light touch ran down Maeve's spine as she washed the wounds, and each new caress caused both pleasure and pain, warming Maeve in the worst way. She tried to ignore the discomfort as Cassia spread the cool numbing cream across her back and applied the bandages.

"How's your pop?" Maeve said, glad Cassia couldn't see her face. "Happy now, I'll bet."

Cassia stopped bandaging her and sighed. "He is."

"He has no right to tell you who to be friends with." Same fight, different day, but Maeve didn't care anymore. She'd say it until Cassia saw the truth. "You being paired doesn't change things."

"Yes it does." Cassia's voice was firm, and she pressed the last bandage on hard enough to make Maeve wince.

She pulled her suit back up over her shoulders and turned. Cassia's eyes dipped to the exposed line of skin where Maeve's suit was still unzipped. Her gaze ran up her torso and lingered on the dip between her covered breasts.

Maeve's breath quickened. Cassia bit her lip, fair cheeks flaming, and averted her eyes.

Maeve zipped up her suit, pulling it so hard she heard thread tear. "Well, I won't throw away friendships when I get paired."

Cassia started returning her supplies to the cabinet. "It's time I grew up," she said, her voice thick. "I have a husband. I'll be Lead Medic someday, and Jason will be Lead Navigator. I can't... spend my free time drinking in the sublevels with you. It's not responsible."

"We don't have to drink."

"It's not just..." She shook her head. "You know what they say."

"No. What do they say, Cassia?" Maeve stood taller, her anger fading to something like desperation. She knew damn well what everyone said, but she and Cassia had never talked about it before. Not *ever*.

"You know." Cassia shut the cabinet door and paused there, her jaw tight, not looking at Maeve.

"I want to hear it from you."

"They say you're..." Cassia mumbled. "That you're the reason I was forced to pair."

"Who cares? It's not true. Right?"

Cassia didn't respond right away, and Maeve waited, heart pounding.

"No," Cassia said. "Nothing they say is true. I'm not..."

"Deviant? *Broken* like they all say I am?"

Cassia narrowed her eyes. "Stop."

"Who cares what they say, then?" Maeve's brain was screaming at her to shut up, horrified at how vulnerable she sounded. But the darkness was back, threatening to consume her whole. She grabbed Cassia's hand and willed her to be the friend she'd once had.

Cassia yanked her hand away as if Maeve's touch had burned her. She glanced toward the curtain, to the door beyond, like she was worried someone would enter... or like she wanted to escape.

"I care. And my family cares." Cassia's voice cracked. "And I don't need or want this anymore, understand? I'm an adult, not a child. I need to do my duty to the fleet. Jason and I are in the population lottery now. We could be one of the lucky couples to have a healthy child. Maybe it's time you did *your* duty and paired."

Her words were a knife through Maeve's heart, cutting deep. But she recovered... and gave Cassia a proud smile.

"Maybe I will." She pushed past her and stalked back out to the medbay.

Cassia's father was working the station now, and he gave her his usual disapproving stare as she walked past with her head held high.

The other curious medics stopped what they were doing to watch her leave. She had no appetite, so she skipped midmess and headed back to her cubic. Her bunkmates came and went, but the shut privacy panel on her bunk kept anyone from bothering her. As the shift buzzer rang for second shift, she decided to skip that, too. *Fuck consequences.*

Gilly would be Outcast for life, and it was Maeve's fault. Her cowardice had finally hurt someone else—a new half, a girl who had been *much* braver than she'd ever be.

Maeve told herself she wanted control, but like Dritan said... she was just a quitter, too cowardly to do her duty to the fleet and die an honorable death. Too *afraid* to show Cassia how she really felt.

But a sub with twisted desires didn't fit anywhere on this fleet.

She buried her face in her pillow and tried to come up with a surefire way to end her existence with the least amount of pain possible.

Stealing Fenton's card again was an option, but Dritan was onto her and would be watching for that. But there was another way to get herself airlocked.

Treason.

Treason was punishable by death.

Plenty of violations could lead to that sentence, but an easy one was staring her right in the face. All she had to do was physically assault a high-level exec. Head Enforcer Jacobs would be at last mess tonight to announce the draft picks, and Maeve wouldn't mind getting a few punches in for her dead parents.

With the captain there as a witness, Maeve would be labeled a traitor and would probably be airlocked before last mess ended.

Maeve fell asleep with a smile on her lips as she pictured endless space and a red planet spinning on its axis—the promise that this would all be over soon.

Maeve was strangely calm, happy even, when the buzzer went off for last mess. She laced up her boots and joined the tired crowds trudging toward the galley with a spring in her step. As she grabbed her last meal from the cooks, a sense of rightness flowed through her, her mission crystal clear in her mind.

Dritan caught up to her as she sank into her usual seat. "Where were you second shift?

Fenton was pissed. You'll be in the brig to-morrow."

She gave him a small smile. "I'm not really worried about it."

Dritan's brows knit together, and he chewed his lip in frustration. "You're... you're not acting *right*, M. Ya gotta stop it. They'll stick you on grimp if you keep this up. Then you *really* won't be yourself."

Grimp dulled every emotion, but it was highly addictive. The thought of using it had crossed Maeve's mind, but she and Dritan had talked about it before. They'd both rather be dead than living that particular lie.

"Huh. I've never felt *more* like myself." Maeve took a bite of the quin, relishing the taste of it, bland as it was. A person should enjoy their last meal, shouldn't they? It was hard to look Dritan in the eye, knowing what she was about to do, but he'd forgive her. Eventually.

Dritan shook his head, acting irritated, but the rest of their crew showed up, so he dug into his food without responding.

Her crew was quiet and withdrawn, and they ate in silence until a commotion at the door drew their attention. Maeve's pulse sped up as the captain, lead tech, and head enforcer walked through. Miller and Jacobs had holo-gear on this time, each of them wearing a single piece of glasstex over one eye. Maeve's excitement died as a long line of enforcers trailed in behind the execs. They looked alert, stunners at the ready.

Kak. Why hadn't she realized they'd have security when they announced the list? How would she reach Jacobs now?

The three execs went to the dais, and the enforcers formed a half-circle in front of them. No one in the galley sat back down. Instead, at least half the crowd drifted closer, forming a loose ring just outside the line of enforcers.

Maeve pressed her lips together and swung her legs off the bench. She shoved through the gathering crowd to make her way to the front, using her small size to her advantage. She'd made a decision to assault the head enforcer *today*, and she wasn't backing down.

When she reached the line of enforcers, she found herself face-to-face with Fenton. He sneered at her, but she focused on Jacobs, standing behind him.

The captain began another inspirational speech, but the words all ran together, garbled and unintelligible through the red haze Maeve existed in. Nervous energy flooded her system, making her sweat.

Head Enforcer Jacobs stood for everything that was *wrong* with this fleet. Worthy subs got maimed and killed, while the execs lived in luxury. Better food, bigger cubics, different rules, longer lives. Not that she needed *another* reason to hate Jacobs after she'd killed Maeve's parents.

She tried to measure the space between Fenton and the enforcers on either side of him. If she darted forward quickly, she might be small enough to slip through. Then she could hop up on the dais and get some swings in before they stopped her.

The lead tech started reading his list, and a low murmur replaced the crowd's silence as two halfs found out they were going to die tomorrow.

A hand grabbed Maeve's wrist, and she jerked her head to the side to find Dritan there. His presence made her doubt herself, and she grew nauseous from the guilt. Would he suffer if she did this? Maeve shook off Dritan's grasp, her chest heavy with indecision.

The head enforcer moved her fingers through the air as she manipulated the holographic list only she could see.

"Beatrice Maxwell."

"Yoko Himura."

"Dritan Corinth."

"Michael Fitz."

Dritan.

The galley spun around Maeve, and when her gaze landed on Fenton in front of her, his kak-eating grin revealed everything. This was *his* fault. Jacobs kept talking, and Maeve glanced at Dritan. He looked stunned. *Afraid.*

"You're not eighteen," Maeve murmured. "I don't understand."

Dritan tore at his short curls. "My birth records were passed from deka to deka... They've messed them up before... Maybe... I... I don't know."

"We are sending one enforcer down with the team." The head enforcer's voice cut through Maeve's shock. "George Fenton."

Fenton's smirk faded to accommodate his gaping jaw, and he blinked, uncomprehending.

As Jacobs passed the amplifier back to the captain, and he began saying his final words, the grav system seemed to malfunction. Maeve felt like she was floating as she darted forward and slipped between Fenton and the enforcer next to him. Fenton didn't see her coming, too off-balance after his bad news to stop her as she leapt onto the dais beside the head enforcer.

Maeve clenched her fists tight, facing Jacobs, and the whole room went quiet. Blood pounded in her ears, her rage begging to be set free, to be unleashed on this woman, as if hurting her would make it all better.

But Maeve's body betrayed her.

The words fell from her mouth like a bad hand of chips, tossed on a table for everyone to see.

"You've made a mistake," she said, barely hearing the words leaving her own mouth. "Dritan Corinth isn't eighteen yet. But I am. We have the same training and are on the same crew. I volunteer to go in his place."

CHAPTER FIVE

Galley conversation erupted into a roar. Or maybe that was just Maeve's pulse in her ears.

The head enforcer recovered from her surprise and ordered the enforcers to stay in formation. "What's your name?"

"Maeve Vasquez."

Jacobs inclined her head slightly, and the lump in Maeve's throat threatened to choke her. What had she just done?

"You may take Dritan Corinth's place." Jacobs gestured to the nearest enforcer, and he guided Maeve back off the dais.

She could barely hear, barely see as the captain continued his final speech, and the crowd began to disperse. Every muscle in her body seemed paralyzed as she stared down at her hands.

The crowd cleared, and when she looked up again, she found Dritan, the rest of their crew arrayed behind him. They all had new respect in their eyes... except for Dritan. He wasn't making any effort to hide his pain this time.

The urge to escape washed over Maeve, and she ran past them all. Dritan followed her into the corridor and grabbed her by the shoulder, spinning her to face him.

"It was supposed to be *me*." Dritan squeezed her shoulders tighter. "Fuck, M. Why?!"

Maeve jumped at his sudden outburst and glanced around as people in the corridor stopped whatever they were doing to stare at them.

"Answer me." Dritan got closer, pushing her into the wall. "Why do you have a death wish?"

"The correct response is *thank you*." She pushed him away hard, and he let her go with a look of defeat.

She took off at a fast clip down the corridor, her blood rushing to her head. Her death wish hadn't included a fiery ending. All she'd wanted to do was control when she died... and choose the least painful way possible.

What have I done?

Fenton didn't have a monopoly on illegal hooch. Maeve's stash was hidden in an empty storage cubic in an abandoned sector on P2. And that's what she needed right now—a drink.

The stairwell was still full of subs and techs as she entered it, but she slipped between them all, shoving through to get where she was going. Curses floated around her, but she ignored them. The crowd dissipated at zero deck, and Maeve caught her breath before jogging down to the abandoned sector on P2.

Most of the lume bars had been recycled there, and many of the panels had been stripped away, revealing dead and burned out components in the walls. Every machine there had been stripped for parts, so except for the hum of the power core, it was blissfully silent.

When she got to the repurposed storage cubic, she pulled out the fermenting quin alcohol and poured some of it into her canteen. Someone had lifted a stained cot from recyc ages ago, and as Maeve sank down on it, legs shaky, the door slid open.

Dritan stormed into their spot without meeting her eyes or saying a word and grabbed some of the hooch. He leaned against the wall and sucked it down, his face twisted with anger. She'd never seen him this mad. Maeve took a long draught, and it burned like fire all the way down her throat.

He was clearly trying to think of a solution to a problem he couldn't fix, which is what he always did. She went numb as she drained her canteen, the effect of the hooch intensifying with every sip. Volunteering had been the right thing to do. The fleet needed colonists like Dritan, colonists who believed in duty and a better world. They didn't need her.

"Sit down." She patted the cot. "I *volunteered*. You aren't eighteen, and they won't take my name off the list now. You can't fix this."

He chugged another mouthful and didn't look at her.

She dropped her empty canteen to the cot and went to stand in front of him.

"I can't fight it anymore." Maeve's voice cracked, and she hated how she sounded. Dritan finally met her eyes, and she licked her lips, forcing herself to continue. "Ever since my parents... Since Cassia. You don't understand. There's this... darkness."

"You're not *alone*. You don't think I've felt what you're feeling?"

She stared at him, not knowing what to say. He'd had a rough start in life, but he'd always acted so optimistic. "I... I don't know how else to escape it."

Dritan took another chug and didn't answer, just stared back at her, judging her with his intense eyes until Maeve couldn't take it anymore. She returned to the cot, twisting her canteen in her hands over and over as the long silence stretched between them.

Dritan pushed off the wall and grabbed her canteen from her grasp. He refilled both their bottles, then sank down close beside her.

Maeve took her canteen from him with mumbled thanks.

She forced a laugh to fill the silence. "So. Did you see Fenton's face when they called his name?"

The barest hint of a smile crossed Dritan's lips. "I can't say I felt sorry for him."

"That's what he gets for setting you up."

Dritan looked at her, a strange expression on his face.

"What?"

"The way you stood up to him during first shift... I've never seen you act like that before."

Maeve looked down at her distorted reflection in the canteen's scratched metal. "Well, I went to see Gilly after. She lost part of her arm."

"But she's *alive*," he said. "You'd be dead if you'd gone in there. You know it. Everyone knows it."

"It should have been me."

Dritan shook his head with a frown. "When you went to medbay..."

"Yeah?"

"You see Cass?"

The darkness broke through Maeve's wall again, and her chest grew heavy with it. "Yeah. Same as before. Said I needed to bugger off. Grow up, do my *duty*. She said I should pair." She nudged Dritan playfully. "So how 'bout it, Corinth? If I live through this, wanna pair with me? You're the only one dumb enough to stick by my side."

Dritan hesitated, then ran a calloused finger along her cheek. Her brows went up in surprise from the gentle touch. His hazel eyes were soft, and the look in them...

"And you're the only one who volunteered," he said, his voice husky. "The only one."

She broke eye contact and let out a nervous laugh. "Is that a no?"

Dritan took another drink, then gave her a small smile. "I'm not what you want."

"Doesn't matter what I want, does it?" *Kak.* Wrong thing to say. Why did she always say the wrong thing?

Dritan's eyes gave his feelings away, even as he tried to hide them. Maeve had fooled around with some of the other guys—experimenting, trying so hard to *feel* something with them. But never once had she crossed that line with Dritan. She'd always known he cared too much. She'd just tried to pretend that didn't matter.

Conflicting emotions tore through her. She loved Dritan... as a friend. But she couldn't imagine being forced to pair with anyone else, to share that sort of intimacy with any other man. But she'd probably die tomorrow anyway.

Her eyes burned as she took another gulp of alcohol. "What I mean is..." she said, her voice small. "You're my best friend. If it isn't you, then... who?"

He wrapped an arm around her and drew her close. She cuddled into his chest, her eyes welling with the tears she'd been fighting to banish all day. What had it cost him, watching her love someone else, watching her want to *die* while still being there for her day after day?

Dritan stroked her short hair, running his fingers through it. "Just come back," he said, his voice rough. "Come back to me, and ask me again... I'll say yes."

Her tears broke through at his words, but she blinked them away as he held her. If she could admit the truth about Dritan, then it was time she admitted the truth about herself... that she couldn't love him, or any man, the way other women loved men. And Dritan deserved something *real*, not whatever she could offer him, even if she somehow did manage to survive Soren. She scooted up and rested her cheek on his shoulder.

"Nah. Don't wait for me," she said in his ear. "I want you to fall for some other girl and be happy. Win the lotto. Make a cute little Corinth baby. Promise me that?"

He nodded.

"Promise."

He paused for a long moment. "Yeah. I promise."

"Now how 'bout another drink?"

Maeve and Dritan stayed up for another hour, working on the hooch, until they were drunk enough to laugh and relive old memories, like the time Fenton pissed himself in front of everyone after a night of drinking a particularly bad batch of bootleg. At some point, they drank themselves to sleep, and they didn't wake until the first shift buzzer sounded.

They solemnly marched upstairs to change and visit the lavs, and by the time they reached singles sector, it was empty, everyone already at first mess. When they were done, they returned to the main stairwell.

"Do you want me to come with you to the hangar bay?" Dritan asked, his voice strained. She shook her head, and he wrapped her in a strong hug. "You can get through this. I know you can."

"Sure I can. And lucky for you, I'm taking Fenton with me. Try not to celebrate too much."

He laughed. "You stay safe. You still owe me a game of chips. I expect you to make good on that when you get back." Dritan's eyes were glistening, barely. This was getting dangerously close to tear-territory.

She winked at him. "A better world awaits, right?"

"A better world awaits," he echoed.

Saying good-bye seemed too much like admitting she was about to die, so she set her shoulders and hurried down the steps, leaving Dritan behind.

The stairwell was deserted, and Maeve tried hard not think about burning up in Soren's atmosphere... but failed miserably. As she rounded the final landing before zero deck, she came to a halt, gripping the railing tight.

Cassia stood outside zero deck's entrance in her blue medbay suit, all alone. Her brown hair was mussed, her eyes puffy and red. Seeing her like that shattered Maeve's calm and sent her heart rate skyrocketing.

Cass caught sight of her and jogged up the steps, meeting her on the small landing. "They were talking about a volunteer this morning at mess. And it was you. You volunteered." An accusation, not a question.

"Yep. I did."

Cassia grabbed Maeve by the shoulders and squeezed hard, her face crumpling. "Don't you get it? They're all going to die. All of them. I can get you off the mission. Let me try talking to Zephyr... "

"You wanna use the captain's daughter like that?" Maeve pushed Cassia away and crossed her arms over her racing heart. "If it's not me, it'll be someone else. Why are you *here*?"

Cassia didn't answer, just stared her down with those deep blue eyes, her hands in tight fists, her breasts rising and falling with each breath.

"You made it pretty clear yesterday how you really feel." Maeve tried to inch around her. "I'm gonna be late."

Cassia grabbed Maeve's arm. "I *do* care."

Maeve hesitated, feeling sick. "I gotta go."

"I care," Cass said. "I just think... that it's not right."

"What's not right?" Maeve whirled to face her and stepped closer, backing Cass into the wall. They were so close, she could feel Cassia's warm, rapid breath on her cheek. "Say it."

Sparks danced between them, electric in the silence, and Cass glanced up the empty stairwell nervously.

Maeve was teetering on the edge, about to fall over. This felt too daring, here in the open, but she'd never come so close to acting. Had never come so close to forcing Cassia to speak the unspoken. What did she have to lose now?

"What's. Not. Right?" Maeve repeated, her voice husky.

"It's not right..." Cassia licked her lips. "It's not right that they're sending *you*. That you volunteered."

Maeve let all her feelings show on her face. "Is that all?" Her hand moved of its own volition, and she grazed Cassia's full lips with her thumb.

They trembled beneath her gentle touch.

Cassia's breathing went shallow. "This thing between us isn't... normal. It's not... real."

Maeve took a deep breath and cast aside her fear, knowing this might be the only chance she got. She pressed her lips to Cassia's, savoring the soft, smooth warmth of them. Cassia went rigid for a moment, then relaxed into the kiss, returning it.

New sensations raced through Maeve, different from anything she'd ever felt with the boys. She wrapped an arm around Cassia, pulling her closer, running a hand down her lower back, seeking her hips, then the gentle swell of her breasts beneath her suit. Cass didn't try to stop her.

The new, heady feelings were suffocating, so intense Maeve felt herself losing control. Then the fear seized her—that she'd just crossed a line she could never uncross, and she pulled away. Both of them were breathing hard, and Cassia's hand went to her lips, her expression a mixture of shock and open desire.

She feels it.

She feels what I feel.

The realization made Maeve bold. "Was that real enough for you?"

Cassia met her gaze, and her cheeks reddened. "Yes."

Heat radiated through Maeve's chest at that single word, and then Cassia leaned in to kiss her with a hunger she hadn't had before. She led the way, opening her mouth to find Maeve's tongue. Desire and desperation heated the space between them as the precious minutes they had left slipped away.

The buzzer sounded, signaling an end to first mess, and voices filled the stairwell. They broke apart, breathless.

"I have to go." Maeve searched Cassia's face, desperately memorizing every curve, every line.

"Then you have to come back."

Maeve let out a laugh. "After that? It's probably better for us both if I don't."

"No. It's better for me if you *do*." Cassia looked like she was about to cry.

Pain tore through Maeve at the devastation on Cassia's beautiful face. "Even if I come back... We can't..."

"We'll just have to patch that panel when it fails," Cassia said firmly, using a sublevel phrase she'd learned from Maeve.

The crowds reached them, colonists flowing around them on the way to work, shooting them irritated looks for blocking the landing.

"Good-bye, Cassia," Maeve said.

Cass nodded, blinking back tears, then ran up the stairs, back to Exec level and her other life.

Maeve walked down the stairs and through the zero deck doors. As she made her way to the hangar bay, she felt lighter than she had in a long time.

Whatever happened next, she felt ready to face it.

CHAPTER SIX

As Maeve entered the hangar bay, she slowed to take it all in. She'd never been in here before—had never had a reason to be.

The transport ships were docked in even rows, but there were far fewer ships than docking bays. A small group of subs and techs had gathered near an active transport at the center of the bay.

Flight crews swarmed around it, getting everything ready. The sound of the engines warming up echoed off the high beams of the bay, and the pungent scent of the fuel stung Maeve's nostrils. An ancient, dinged infinity symbol was engraved along one panel, just like on the cargo ships the *Moscow* used to distribute supplies.

But these were different and much smaller. The ramp had been lowered, and she glimpsed the cockpit, with room for two pilots, and seats lining the interior for a small crew. Flight subs and techs loaded equipment into the cargo hold at the back.

Someone near the wall called out to her, and she stopped walking, disoriented as a flight tech came over.

"You need to scan in," he said.

She clumsily got her shift card out of her pocket and held it against the man's handheld scanner. His eyepiece went from clear to reflective as her data showed up on his holographic display. He twisted his wrist, shutting it off, and gave her a look she couldn't read.

"I have to collect your shift card if you're with the draft."

Of course. Couldn't waste a good piece of plastic. They recyced these cards as soon as a colonist died. Probably weren't even gonna wait to recyc hers.

As she handed him her card, he gave her a respectful nod. "Thank you for volunteering. And good luck."

Maeve grunted a response and headed for the rest of the group, her palms getting damper with each step. More colonists trickled in after her, and finally Head Enforcer Jacobs arrived.

She had bags under her eyes, like she hadn't slept any better than Maeve had.

"Good morning to you all," she said, calling the small group to order. "The *Kyoto* transport is landing as we speak. You'll go next, and the *Perth* transport will follow. The probe data has been programmed into this transport to help lead you safely to the planet's surface. Now we know that the area where you'll be landing has extreme temperatures—swinging from high heat during the day to below freezing at night, but your gear will keep you at a safe temperature. The air is not breathable, so ensure your helmets are intact at all times. I trust you all remember your space gear training, but if you have any questions, ask the flight techs as you suit up.

"The flight crew leading the mission has been well-trained. Their primary objective is to deliver the equipment on that transport safely to the surface." She pointed to the cargo hold of the transport. "If your descent is rocky, they will release the equipment close to the ground, where parachutes will cushion the landing. You need to find the gear, claim it, and get it operational. You've all used this hardware before, during asteroid stops."

Low murmurs filtered through the group, and Maeve kept her eyes on the transport, every muscle tense.

"The *Perth* crew will establish temp shelters that will house all of you," Jacobs continued. "Your flight techs have equipment to help locate them once you land. Communications often lapse during landfall, but as you descend, we should get enough data to ensure more colonists can arrive safely. When we have enough, more transports will follow. The first few weeks will be difficult, but this planet is bound to have some of the resources we need, and you'll be responsible for establishing shelter below ground for incoming miners."

Maeve's mouth went dry at the words, and she glanced to her right, expecting Dritan to be at her side like always. But Fenton stood there instead, his pale skin looking greenish in the bay lights.

She averted her eyes. If they lived... she hadn't thought beyond the dying part. If she survived the landing, she'd still have to survive weeks of dangerous conditions to help establish a settlement for everyone else. Might be better if she *did* die coming through atmo.

"You are all young and strong," Jacobs said, her voice louder now. "We're sending *you* down because you have the best chance of completing the mission and being assets to our flight crew. This is the most important mission you'll ever do. Focus on it at all times, and remember your training."

What training? The flight crew assembled near the transport had all the training. The subs and techs around her... they were just warm bodies. Extra colonists to send out to do the most dangerous work if they reached Soren's surface. *Expendable.* Maeve took a deep breath and pressed her lips together.

The head enforcer gestured to the flight crew leader and then turned back to them. "A better world awaits," she said.

"A better world awaits," the group murmured in automatic response.

Everyone around Maeve looked sick as they were led to the space gear changing area.

Maeve picked a spot next to the lockers and turned her back on the others. She slipped out of her sublevel suit and into the once-white undersuit that went beneath the spacegear. It was too tight against her bandaged wounds, and she grimaced as the cloth chafed them.

While folding up her suit to turn it in, her fingers slid over her pendant. She removed the star-shaped bit of metal from the pocket, her throat tightening at the way the polished metal glinted beneath the lume bars. It was worn around the edges, no longer pointed like it might once have been. Maybe it hadn't been lucky enough to keep her mother safe, but wearing it was like having a part of her parents still with her, so she wouldn't leave it behind.

She dropped the star into the thigh pocket of her undersuit and climbed into the heavier spacegear. The thick fabric of the suit made her sweat even more as a flight tech helped set up her water line and loaded her collar with liquid oxygen packs. He tested her helmet for a proper fit and then had her carry it out to where the rest of them were suited up and boarding.

That's when she realized she was shaking. Badly. The thin barrier of her suit, these little packets of oxygen... they were a joke of a defense against the dangers of open space and a toxic planet.

Fifteen of them were being sacrificed. Eight trained members of the flight crew, two techs, four subs, and one enforcer. Maeve clutched her helmet tightly and strode up the ramp after them and into the transport. The interior seemed cramped now, with sixteen seats in the back and one narrow aisle in between.

The flight tech made her strap in next to Fenton, and the rest of the crew buckled in for their one-way trip. Pale faces, wide eyes, sweat-soaked brows.

This was a fucking suicide mission, and every damn person on this flight knew it. She could see it on their faces, breathe it in the metallic-tasting oxygenated air. She fought down panic as the co-pilot took her helmet from her and secured it above her seat, reassuring her that she'd be able to put it on before they began their descent.

The engines started up, and through the front glasstex, she glimpsed the hangar bay doors sliding open, revealing an expanse of dark space beyond. Maeve held her breath as the ship spooled up and drifted out the door. The pilot angled the thrusters, maneuvering it as they coasted out into open space.

Stars twinkled in the distance, but otherwise it was nothing but blackness. She'd done hull work before, but there wasn't a lot of time to pay attention to the view. Subs accessed the outside of the ship through one of the many airlocks, clung to the hull, did the work, and got back inside. *This* was different.

She could see the *whole* deka as they coasted alongside it, every porthole, every sector of the *London*. When they turned a corner, Maeve sucked in a breath.

Soren appeared before them, so much closer than the last time she'd glimpsed it. Swirling red-orange clouds rotated across the toxic surface, making it seem alive. Alive like no meteor had ever looked.

It was beautiful.

What would it be like to stand on solid ground? To hold soil in her hand? Maeve's eyes burned as she took it in, and she couldn't pull them away as the transport sped up.

When they reached their coordinates, one of the flight techs released his straps and floated down the narrow aisle, helping everyone into their helmets.

The fear mounting within Maeve made it hard to breathe, and she ripped her gaze from Soren, trying to focus on something, anything, else. She watched Bea, the sub who had called her a deev in the galley, fumbling in her suit for a chain. The lack of gravity made it drift upward. It was a bit of scrap metal, symbols etched into it; a cross, a six-pointed star, a crescent—symbols of the old gods. Those gods had died with the Earth, but some colonists still believed.

Bea kissed the pendant, and tears tracked down her face. She wiped them with one gloved hand, and drops of water lifted off her glove and floated through the air.

Maeve's mouth went dry as she locked eyes with Bea, and time slowed for just a moment. They shared a look—a terrifying sort of resigned acceptance—the sort of look only two people who knew they were about to die could share.

It didn't matter what this girl believed or what she didn't believe. It didn't matter how she'd treated Maeve back on the *London*. Two beating hearts, two equally vulnerable bodies that would burn up just the same in atmo when this all went wrong.

The tech floated between them to help Maeve into her helmet, and Maeve let out a breath. When he finished, he returned to his seat, and the pilots commed the flagship *Paragon*.

Maeve's helmet picked it up, since they were all linked together now. The *Kyoto* transport had completed entry, and the *Perth* transport was waiting on the *London* transport to descend.

"What's the status?" the pilot asked. "Did they make it?"

"We lost contact," came a tinny voice from the *Paragon*. "Forwarding revised landing data to your transport for entry."

The line went utterly silent, until quiet muttering filled Maeve's helmet.

"We're all dead. We're all dead. I gotta get out of here."

Maeve recognized the voice right away and turned to her left.

Fenton was hugging himself, sweat streaming down his face under his helmet. "Dead, dead, dead. We're all gonna die."

"If we're all gonna die," Maeve said brightly, "I sure don't want *your* voice to be the last thing I hear. And if you're *wrong*, well, ya better get your kak together. Piss that suit now, and you'll be tastin' it for the next eight hours."

Edgy laughter echoed on the comms, but thankfully Fenton shut up.

And then it was time for the *London*'s transport to descend.

They activated the shielding, and Maeve placed one gloved hand on her thigh where the star pendant was. Terror rushed through her, and she screwed her eyes shut.

This is it.

This was what she'd wanted, wasn't it? She shouldn't be this scared. If she burned up, if they crashed... it would happen fast. Just as fast as if she'd airlocked herself.

I wanted to die. I was ready to end it.

The transport entered the atmosphere with a shudder and started to shake so violently, Maeve's teeth chattered in her head. A loud roar filled her ears, and her head slammed back against her seat, immobilized.

Down, down, down. She sweat freely as the interior temperature seemed to get hotter than a power core.

Ma and Papa. They'd believed in duty just as much as Dritan did. Would they be proud of her for what she'd done, even as she hurtled toward death?

Dritan. His expression when he'd found her in the airlock, the way he'd held her and promised to pair with her, even though he knew the truth about her.

And Cassia. Kissing her, touching her... the look in her blue eyes afterward.

Something snapped on the transport, and a terrible cracking sound reverberated through Maeve's skull. The transport tilted and began to spin sideways. Something was wrong. Very wrong.

The fear was so intense, Maeve wanted to cry, but the velocity made it impossible. She was going to be a coward 'til her last breath.

No.

A coward never would have volunteered for this.

She clung to that thought as they plummeted toward the ground.

She'd made a choice to airlock herself. It had been the coward's way out, but in making that choice, she'd changed.

She chose to stand up to Fenton when his orders were *wrong*. When Dritan was unfairly drafted, she volunteered in his place. And when Cassia came to her, she acted. Exposing herself and being vulnerable with Cassia had terrified Maeve more than the airlock. Yet she'd done it.

Bravery wasn't the absence of fear.

It wasn't controlling every situation and avoiding pain.

And bravery *wasn't* accepting your lot in life without resistance.

You have to take your power back.

She'd done that. Instead of just letting life happen to her, she'd made things happen.

Bravery was making choices and then facing the consequences head-on, all while *knowing* the outcome was uncertain. Fear didn't make her a coward. Letting her lot in life dictate the course of it had.

And she'd *chosen* to live or die on this mission.

I'm not a coward.

I'm brave.

"Dropping... the... gear." The pilot's voice cut in and out.

A stream of light peeked through the rivets across from Maeve, and her heart nearly stopped as the bright light illuminated the colonists on that side. She locked eyes with Bea again. Hers were enormous, terrified like the rest of them.

Nothing Maeve could do. Nothing anyone could do.

The panel across from Maeve tore off and took six seats with it.

Bea was gone.

Six of them were *gone*.

Alarms erupted in the ship as it spun, and on every stomach-lurching rotation, Maeve glimpsed the soil through the gaping hole.

The dim, reddish surface of the planet rushed up at them. Red sand. Rocks. Too fast. The pilots shouted something, and the ship wobbled and almost righted itself... but didn't. Couldn't.

Maeve didn't know much about flying, but she knew they couldn't slow down in time. She kept her eyes open. If death wanted to take her, she'd see its face before she surrendered.

The transport shuddered forward and leveled slightly before smashing into the sand.

Maeve's head snapped back against the seat.

Bright lights. Alarms. And deafening screams that weren't her own.

Nothingness beckoned, and Maeve fought until she couldn't any more. Then the darkness swallowed her whole.

CHAPTER SEVEN

When Maeve's eyes opened, the world still spun. She nearly puked from the vertigo but managed to hold it back. Puke in spacegear once, you never made that mistake again.

Her vision cleared, and she focused on a sphere of light reflecting off metal. The cargo hold door. A figure in spacegear was trying to pry the door open, but he seemed to be at a strange angle...

Maeve looked straight ahead, and the place where Bea and the others had been was filled with dark sand. The transport had landed on its side.

Two colonists remained in the opposite aisle, and Maeve nearly threw up again at the sight of them. Crushed skulls, faces barely recognizable. Their helmets had smashed on impact, and blood coated everything, even their suits. At least they'd probably died instantly.

Nothing but silence from the cockpit—two bodies up front twisted at awkward angles. Dead. For sure.

A crack of light entered the cabin as the survivor succeeded in making the cargo hold door move.

Clear head. Determination. Maeve had to find her voice and get out of here.

"Help." The single word was barely a whisper, and her comm probably hadn't picked it up. She fumbled with her straps, trying to release them. With strength she shouldn't have had, she got her fingers to comply and pressed down on the clasps. They let go, and she crashed to the sand below.

Maeve checked her oxygen levels. Holding firm. No tears in her suit. It was hard to breathe for some reason, but she was alive. *Maybe I got some lucky genes of my own af-ter all.*

The figure ahead whirled and stumbled over. "I thought you... thought you were all dead," he slurred.

Maeve saw her own reflection in the man's helmet, but then her eyes focused on his face behind the glass, then the wound on his head. His hair was caked with blood, and she traced its path as it flowed down his cheek. Some part of her brain recognized him as the flight tech who had strapped her in. His helio moved, and it lit up the two subs above them that had been sitting to Maeve's right. Their heads slumped forward, arms and legs hang-ing down limply. More blood. Lots of it. And cracked helmets. Definitely dead.

"Gotta... we gotta get out." The tech ex-tended a hand.

Maeve took his arm and scrambled to her feet, hissing in a breath as something stabbed her deep in the ribs. She gritted her teeth to help the tech pry the cargo hold door the rest of the way open, and light flooded the space.

As the tech squeezed over the edge, Maeve began to count.

Six ripped from the ship during the landing.

Four dead in the back. Both pilots dead in the cockpit.

Two alive.

Fourteen.

One left.

She spun, looking back. Fenton was still strapped into the seat to the left of where she'd been.

"Oxygen tank's leaking," the tech said from the hold, his voice crackling over the comm.

Maeve had to climb on top of the dead techs to get to Fenton, and she tried not to think about what she stood on as their broken bodies squished beneath her boots.

When she reached Fenton, she tapped his helmet. Still intact. His eyes opened, and for a moment, his dilated pupils found hers and seemed to light with recognition. But then his lids slid shut again. *Alive.* Three of them alive.

Blue sparks lit up the ceiling, jumping from exposed wiring, and she jerked back. No fires yet, but if the oxygen was leaking...

"There's another survivor," she said.

But the tech was gone, and he didn't answer. Maeve glanced toward the open cargo hold, to the bright light, to freedom, *to life*. And then back up to the sparking wires and Fenton.

He was a piece of kak, but he was one of them, and he didn't deserve to die like this. Maeve had to stand on tiptoes, almost losing her balance on the unstable bodies beneath her boots. But she found the clasps on Fenton's harness and struggled to press them, dizziness sweeping over her. Something in her chest was wrong, painful if she moved too fast, making it hard to breathe.

She fumbled, panic rising within her as more sparks jumped from the wires. Finally, one strap gave. As Fenton's harness let loose, his unconscious body fell on top of her, pinning her to the mangled flight tech beneath them. She let out a grunt and hauled him off her.

It took every last ounce of her dwindling strength to pull Fenton toward the light. Her chest screamed at her to stop as she hauled his body over the threshold and into the cargo hold. A loud hissing sound filled her ears, even through her thick helmet. The tech had been right—the oxygen was escaping, the tank cracked.

The tech lurched back into the hold and pulled a case away from one wall.

"Help," Maeve gasped.

The tech narrowed his eyes in confusion, like he'd forgotten she was there, but then he dropped the case and helped her lug Fenton out into the blinding light of the planet. The comm line filled with their panting as they half-carried, half-dragged Fenton a few yards away from the crash site.

They collapsed on the ground, and Maeve squinted against the harsh light, trying to see. The pain in her ribs faded away as her eyes adjusted, and a lightness flooded her. Elation stole away the pain.

The star in this system looked like a *helio*, streaming light through a red-tinged sky.

A sky. No observation deck could compare to what a *sky* looked like. Expansive, enormous, filling up everything as far as Maeve could see. She flopped over on her side and took a handful of the soil, watching as the fine dust ran through her fingers, turned her glove red. Like asteroid dust, or metal dust, but... different.

She looked out over the land, breathing too fast. A mound of smooth rock rose tall on one side of her, but everywhere else...

Sand. Miles and miles of it, dotted with more stone formations. Huge rocks rose far in the distance, forming chains so high she couldn't imagine climbing over them.

So beautiful. The scene was so painfully beautiful, in a way the dark expanse of space couldn't compete with. A lump formed in Maeve's throat. It felt like *home*, like she'd been living a false life surrounded by metal, and she'd finally found truth.

This was what everyone dreamed of. Solid ground beneath them, air and sky above. No.

Not this. But *like* this, only *green* with oxygen and plentiful water.

"We're way off course," the tech's slurred words broke through her elation. "The gear. Sandstorms. A storm'll tear us apart if we don't get to shelter. I... the tracker." The tech got to his feet. "We need the tracker to find... *Perth* transport."

"Wait," Maeve said weakly, sitting up. "The oxygen tank's leaking. It could blow."

"Have to get the tracker." He jogged away, wavering on his feet, not moving in a straight line, but he made it back to the twisted hulk of their transport.

A few cases lay scattered in the sand, and Maeve glanced at Fenton beside her, at his chest rising and falling with breath, then back at the transport. She got up, gasping from the pain, and dragged Fenton another few feet through the sand until they were both behind the smooth rocks. Then she fell to her knees, panting, watching the transport for sign of the tech.

Hurry.

They needed him. He'd been trained for this, knew how to use the tracker, how to survive until the next wave arrived. Without him...

Relief coursed through Maeve as she glimpsed a flash of white at the end of the hold. The tech stumbled back outside, tripping through the wreckage with a black case in his arms.

"I got—"

A flash of fire leapt from the cargo hold and ignited the tech's suit.

Fuck. Maeve sank down behind the rocks, curling into herself. The explosion was deafening.

All she heard was a high-pitched ringing as shards of twisted metal flew past and landed in the sand, smoking.

When her hearing returned, she waited a few minutes in the silence, then got to her feet and scrambled back toward the remains of the transport. The tech's body lay off to the side, mangled, his spacegear blackened in places. One of his legs was missing. She swallowed back bile and looked for the case he'd gone in for.

It was laying a few yards away, and she limped in that direction and sank down on her knees in front of it. Her thoughts were a chaotic jumble, and the adrenaline surging through her made her hands shake so badly, she couldn't get the case open.

Clear head, M. Focus.

She took a deep breath and tried to pretend this was a job in the sublevels. It just happened to be a job with a kak survival rate.

She tried to wipe the sweat off her face, but her glove met glass. The drops slid into her eyes, burning them.

"Get the tracker working, find a medkit, wake up Fenton, get to the *Perth* transport." She recited her tasks over and over to herself, until her hands steadied and she could open the case.

The gear inside resembled a handheld shift card scanner, but with a 2D display instead of a hologear hookup. Maeve had never used any of that, but how   hard could it be?

She fumbled around with the buttons until the display blinked on. A blue dot appeared on a grid, and she stood up and walked back toward the smooth rocks. The dot moved with her and stopped when she stopped.

The scanner was the blue dot. She tapped some of the commands, but nothing happened. Fear rose in her again, but she repeated her task list in her mind to calm herself.

She hit another command, and the grid got smaller. A red dot appeared, blinking at the far edge of it. She tapped the red dot, and a list of numbers appeared followed by a single word.

PERTH.

The *Perth* transport.

A laugh bubbled out of Maeve's mouth. *Task one complete. Task two, medkit.* The tracker had an armband attachment, so she slid it around her bulky suit. Then she sucked in another pained breath and searched for the helix symbol among the debris around her. *There.* A twisted piece of hull, engraved with one half of the infinity symbol. The helix and triquetra symbol peeked out at her from a case buried beneath it.

Maeve dug it out and, with shaking hands, readied a full-body painmod vial and twisted it onto the medport on her suit. It triggered the injection, and the sharp pain in her ribs faded as most of her body went numb. Getting back to Fenton was the easiest part. She injected him with a vial of Perc.

His eyes snapped open, and he jerked into sitting position, gasping and holding his abdomen in pain. "My stomach..." Then he noticed their surroundings, eyes wide and glassy. "We're here. We're alive."

She grabbed him by the shoulders to make him stay still, then injected painmod into his port to balance out the Perc.

He winced, but the crazed look in his eyes faded. "I think I broke something." He patted his abdomen.

"Your oxygen levels?"

He looked down at the packs in his suit. "Holding." He stumbled to his feet, and went still when he saw the wreckage. "Where is everyone?"

"Dead. All of 'em."

His eyes narrowed, squinting at her. "In the transport... did you...?"

"Yeah, I saved your stupid ass." Maeve shoved the medkit into Fenton's arms. "Come on. We got a long walk."

CHAPTER EIGHT

The hot sand seemed to waver before them, and Maeve squinted against the bright light, trying and failing to gauge how far they needed to travel. Endless red stretched before them... no sign of the *Perth* transport.

How far? The damn tracker didn't say how far away the red dot was, though it probably would if she hit enough buttons. But then she risked screwing up the display and losing the map again.

One step. Then another. Her suit seemed to get heavier with each minute that passed. Was it the gravity here? The weight on her shoulders felt so heavy, like it was trying to convince her to fall to the ground and just give up. Her gear was keeping her about as cool as any job near the power core, and her inner suit was soaked through with sweat already. She took a sip of water from the recyc tube. Tasted of piss.

But at least she was alive.

"I don't see nothin'," Fenton panted beside her. "I bet you can't even read that thing."

"I can."

"What if that's not even the *Perth* transport?"

"It *is*."

"Yeah?" Fenton scowled at her. "Well they're probably all dead, too."

"Don't *make* me regret saving you." Maeve forced herself to walk faster to leave him behind.

She *wanted* Fenton to answer with his usual caustic reply, but he didn't. Her whole world had fallen apart around her, had been turned upside down to the point where she'd saved *Fenton*, and now he was following her lead.

But the worst part was that Fenton was right. What if it was the *Perth* transport, but there was no shelter, no supplies? What if they *did* find a disaster like the crash they'd just left? They could walk all that way just to run out of oxygen and die before help arrived.

The walk seemed to go on for hours, and maybe it did. Nothing broke up their journey through endless sand. No transport beckoned to them in the distance. But, still, the red dot slowly grew closer on the grid. Something was out there.

The pain in Maeve's chest was coming back, a slow burn that would only get worse. She was about to stop to shoot up more pain-mod when the first shudder vibrated through her boots. She and Fenton both froze, and when the ground shook beneath them a second time, Fenton cried out. The third tremor ripped violently through the land beneath them, knocking them both down.

Vibrations rattled Maeve's bones, shook her brain as the surface danced before her. Like going through the atmo all over again. She gripped at the shifting sand on her hands and knees, teeth chattering in her skull, sour bile inching up her throat.

Just as suddenly as it began, it stopped.

"What the fuck was that? What the *fuck*?" Fenton's high-pitched whine pierced her aching head, and she stumbled back to her feet and lunged at him, slamming a fist into his chest and knocking him flat on his back.

She straddled him, pinning his shoulders to the ground. When he glared back, she saw *shame* in his eyes. *Good.*

"I swear on the ancestors," she growled, "I will shoot you up with grimp *and* painmod right now, and I *will* leave you here to die."

"Get off me, glitch." His strained voice crackled through the comm. "I'm an *enforcer*."

She shifted her weight to his injured abdomen and dug her knee in. He let out a yelp as she leaned close, until their helmets were inches apart. "Do you see any ships? There *are* no enforcers on Soren. It's just me and you. And *I* have the tracker."

She climbed off of him and grabbed another vial of painmod for herself. Another small tremor shifted the ground beneath her, but she kept her balance this time and started walking. More tremors vibrated through her boots, but as she walked, they became fewer and farther between.

She never looked back, but Fenton's heavy breathing filled her comm, letting her know he still followed.

As she walked, the strange wavering look of the air before her cleared, and she glimpsed a tall rock formation up ahead. Going around it would take them off course, but those stones were too high to climb.

And the sun's light was fading. It was blistering hot on this planet, of that she had no doubt, but as night fell, it would drop to freezing. Her suit should protect her, but how would she find her way through the dark? Maeve glanced at her oxygen levels as she reached the formation. Half-gone. Not good. She'd breathed away more than half her allotted life.

The time for giving up and dying had passed. For some reason, she'd been spared when everyone else had died. She wasn't about to give up and die so close to rescue, suffocating here. She took another sip of sour water and tried to push the thoughts away.

After a long trek along the rock line, she and Fenton finally reached the end and turned the corner. They were met by a thick haze of red. Fine grains of sand whipped through the air, making it hard to see.

She glanced down at her tracker and adjusted course. The red dot looked very close. They could be yards away... or miles.

"Vasquez." Fenton panted.

The haze parted ahead for just for a moment, and she squinted, peering through the dust. A glint of metal, a small structure ahead. Metal tubes in front, drilled deep into the soil. *The soil sampler.* Maeve's chest expanded, and new energy coursed through her as she hurried forward through the haze. "It's a temp shelter! We found them."

"Vasquez."

"Come on."

"Maeve!" Fenton's voice was urgent. "What the fuck is that?"

She glanced at him in alarm and then looked up where he was pointing. In the distance, a swirling wall of solid *red* was quickly approaching the shelter... and them. Maeve's throat constricted, her mind returning to what the tech had slurred. *Sandstorms. A storm'll tear us apart.*

"Run." Adrenaline shot through Maeve, offering strength. She dropped the bulky medkit—it would only slow her down—and tapped the star pendant at her thigh for good luck. Then she tried to sprint.

Tried. Every step was a fight against nature, a fight against the gravity on this planet, a fight to make her exhausted and injured body respond. Her eyes burned as she fought to move faster. She wouldn't die—not this close to shelter.

Fenton pulled alongside her, then ahead. The wall of red grew closer, red dust whirling in chaos, heading straight for them.

Maeve's heart raced, and she ran harder. She let out a muffled scream as the pain from her ribs suddenly reappeared, her last shot of painmod fading out.

The sandstorm's roar permeated the glasstex of her helmet, a dull roar coming to eat her alive. Fenton was yards ahead of her now, and she was all alone, dust swirling around her.

It was so hard to breathe. Without wanting to, Maeve slowed. She doubled over in pain, sucking in breath. "I can't..." she gasped.

An unintelligible voice crackled through the comm. Not Fenton's. A woman's. Maeve lurched forward, peering through the dust, and made out a figure emerging from the structure.

Fenton reached her, and they both disappeared inside.

No. Maeve sucked in a breath and fought against her pain, sweat pouring down her face as she put one boot in front of the other. She'd never make it in time.

The storm was almost on her, and the door still yards away, when two colonists emerged from the structure and ran for her.

She nearly collapsed as their arms wrapped around her, and they dragged her through the door ahead. They bolted it shut behind them, and as she fell to her knees inside the small, dim structure, her eyes adjusted to the dark space. She nearly sobbed with relief. Solid metal panels, panels made on the *London*, curved above their heads, and thick rods had been driven deep into the soil to secure the shelter.

Cases were stacked along one wall, and two helios bobbed beside colonists in space-gear, illuminating the faces of the survivors. *Four.* Only four survivors besides Maeve and Fenton.

"We're from the *London* transport." Fenton's voice crackled on the comm. "Only two of us. You it?"

"Yes," the woman said. "Lost our transport. Tank got busted."

"The *Kyoto* transport?"

"No sign. Burned up on the way down."

Silence on the line.

The storm hit, enveloping them with its rage, rocking the structure back and forth like its only purpose was to tear it from the soil. The tiny grains buffeted them, pelting the metal.

Please hold. It had to hold.

"It might be a few more hours," the woman said, talking loudly into the comms, so they could hear over the roar. "The other transports won't come down in this."

She was talking about the next wave. Maeve checked her oxygen again. Two to three hours left at most. She should have recovered the packs from the colonists who had died. But she couldn't change them out here... a transport with a functioning oxygen tank might have given them more hours than they had now.

Maeve curled up, grunting against the pain in her ribs and the lesser sharp pain of the wounds on her back. She glanced at Fenton, but he was lying on the ground with his eyes closed.

As the storm raged on, the woman and another man went to a machine at the back of the shelter.

"Busted up. Can't be fixed."

They chatted for a while longer, and Maeve listened through her haze of pain. "You guys got any painmod?" she finally asked.

The man closest to her, the one who looked injured, fumbled in a case beside him and rolled a vial toward her. She injected herself, and as the numbness took her, she could breathe again.

Somehow, even with the steady pelting of sand against metal, she slipped into restless sleep.

When she woke, it was because the ground beneath her was moving again. It jolted, throwing her into the wall. The sandstorm still roared around them, and the metal structure shook even harder. This planet was a fucking nightmare.

When the shaking stopped, voices erupted on the comms, everyone talking at once, their complaints melding together.

Maeve sat up, her head aching as she checked her oxygen. Her stomach clenched. Less than an hour left now, and the storm was still going.

The conversation died down, and she glanced at Fenton in his corner, hate writhing

in her chest. Why had she saved him? Six survivors. Six out of forty-five. Why did it have
to be him? He didn't even *deserve* to live.

Disgust made Maeve get up and stumble
to the other side of the space, where the two
techs still focused on the machine they'd
been working on earlier.

One of them looked up at her, his face sag-
ging with exhaustion.

Maeve sunk down beside him. It was a soil
analysis machine like they had on the *London*.
"Broken?"

The other tech nodded, and Fenton walked
over to them and leaned against the wall.
Maeve inched away from him, wishing he'd
go away.

"If anyone can fix that, it's Vasquez," Fenton said.

"Who?"

Maeve's brows shot up at his words, and
the other two looked at her. The man shoved
the workcase toward Maeve and backed away.
"It's busted. You think it can be fixed, have at
it."

He sank down against the wall, giving up.

Maeve swallowed and took another glance at her oxygen, panic rising within her. She was going to die here. After everything... this was where it ended.

She tore at the machine's panel with clumsy gloved hands. The task calmed her mind, steadied her hands and nerves as she assessed the damage. Crushed components— that was the issue. So she got to work, replacing the wires and substituting others from the dented workcase. The rhythm of the job soothed her, and she forced herself not to check her oxygen again.

As she was twisting the final wires together, the pelting on the shelter ceased. Everyone exchanged glances at the sudden silence, and one of them cracked open the door. Thick dust rushed in, coating them in the stuff, but the man let out a whoop. The storm had passed and was moving away from them.

Maeve let out a little choked laugh and finished her job. The interface activated, and the man who had been working on it earlier flashed her a tired smile. "Good work, sub."

The woman headed outside with the other uninjured tech, and they came back with a vial of soil, sampled from deep within the planet's crust.

Maeve got out of the way as the tech checked the soil sample, then slowly fed the vial into the slot for analysis. The scanner turned on, and Maeve waited, barely able to breathe. From her injury or fear, she wasn't sure. Had any of this been worth it? Would this planet even have what the fleet needed?

The analysis took several long minutes, and they all sank back down on the soil, exhausted, heads hanging low. Maeve kept vigil with them and tried to breathe slower, to use up less of her quickly diminishing oxygen levels.

When the results came back, the tech read them aloud.

Maeve's stomach dropped with every name. A long list, all common elements.

But then the tech stopped. They all looked up at her, and she returned her gaze to the display.

"*Martisium*," she said.

The metal they needed to build the jump gate.

Maeve stumbled to her feet, checking the display for herself.

There it was, among the rest. *Martisium*.

"A better world awaits," Maeve found herself saying.

"A better world awaits," five voices came back.

Maeve pushed through the door, back onto the windswept red plain. She stared up at the sky, still hazy with red dust, then fell to the soil. Breathing hard, she took a fresh handful of it in her hand, letting it run through her gloved fingers and fall back to the ground.

Over and over, she let the fine grains fall, dancing in the air as they joined the rest.

Martisium.

The fleet could jump.

She stared up into the sky just in time to see lights peeking through the haze. A transport, landing in the distance. Then more lights, in another direction.

It was the second wave. With supplies. With *oxygen*.

Maeve's chest lightened, and she threw another handful of sand into the air and watched it fall. Tears streamed down her face as she dug both hands deep into the soil.

Hope. Soren meant hope.

I want to survive.

I'm brave enough to live this life.

A better world awaits. And Maeve believed.

LEGACY CODE
SOUNDTRACK

Autumn Kalquist and music producer Freya Wolfe have created an official soundtrack for Legacy Code.

Please visit **AutumnKalquist.com** to find out how you can listen to "Crash and Burn", a song inspired by this book.

"CRASH AND BURN" LYRICS

3, 2, 1
You are cleared for landing.

Chorus:
Crash and burn
Crash and burn
Crash and burn
(3, 2, 1)

Verse 1:
We burn so bright, we hide, and we fight.
Fallin' off the edge, I'm in too deep.

We burn so bright, we hide, and we fight.
Darkness swallows me, and I can't breathe.

Pre-chorus:
Fell too far
Laid bare, naked, and open
Fell too hard
Bloody, bare, and broken

Chorus
Crash and burn
Crash and burn
Crash and burn
(3, 2, 1)

Verse 2:
We fly so high, we rise, and we lie.
Above it all, you set me free.
We fly so high, we rise, and we lie.
A better world—make me believe.

Pre-chorus:
Fell too far
Laid bare, naked, and open

Fell too hard
Bloody, bent, and broken

Chorus:
Crash and burn
Crash and burn
Crash and burn
(3, 2, 1)

Bridge:
Maybe we'll crash and burn.
Don't matter what they say.
On the edge, I'm falling over.
But my world's better when you stay.

Chorus
Crash and burn
Crash and burn
Crash and burn
(3, 2, 1)
Crash and burn
Crash and burn
Crash and burn
(3, 2, 1)

FRACTURED ERA SERIES

DEFECTIVE

LEGACY CODE

ACKNOWLEDGMENTS

Thank you, Juan! As always, I couldn't write these books without your unwavering love and support.

Many thanks to my beta readers, who helped me make this story better:

Alicia Porter, Freya Wolfe, Jamie Blair, and Kevin Stone.

To my editor, Erynn Newman, thank you for being so wonderful to work with.

And to my readers: Your support and enthusiasm for this series mean the world to me! Thank you.